ANIMAL EXPLORERS

REPTILES AND AMPHIBIANS

Michael Leach
and Meriel Lland

Enslow Publishing
101 W. 23rd Street
Suite 240
New York, NY 10011
USA

enslow.com

This edition published in 2020 by Enslow Publishing, LLC
101 W. 23rd Street, Suite 240, New York, NY 10011

Copyright © Arcturus Holdings Ltd 2020

All rights reserved.

No part of this book may be reproduced by any means without the written permission of the publisher.

Cataloging-in-Publication Data

Names: Leach, Michael. | Lland, Meriel.
Title: Reptiles and amphibians / Michael Leach and Meriel Lland.
Description: New York : Enslow Publishing, 2020. | Series: Animal explorers | Includes bibliographical references and index.
Identifiers: ISBN 9781978509955 (library bound) | ISBN 9781978509931 (pbk.) | ISBN 9781978509948 (6 pack)
Subjects: LCSH: Reptiles—Juvenile literature. | Amphibians—Juvenile literature.
Classification: LCC QL644.2 L43 2020 | DDC 597.9—dc23

Printed in the United States of America

To Our Readers: We have done our best to make sure all website addresses in this book were active and appropriate when we went to press. However, the author and the publisher have no control over and assume no liability for the material available on those websites or on any websites they may link to. Any comments or suggestions can be sent by email to customerservice@enslow.com.

Photo Credits:
Every attempt has been made to clear copyright. Should there be any inadvertent omission,
please apply to the publisher for rectification.
Key: b-bottom, t-top, c-center, l-left, r-right

Alamy: 4–5 (Ian Cruickshank), 6–7 (Alejandro Díaz Díez/age fotostock), 10c (All Canada Photos), 17bl (John Cancalosi), 18br (Scott Camazine); FLPA: 8cl (Reinhard Dirscherl), 9cr & 31br (Daniel Heuclin/Biosphoto), 12–13 (Artur Cupak/Imagebroker), 12bl (Paul van Hoof/Minden Pictures), 14–15 (Konrad Wothe/Minden Pictures), 20–21 (Patricio Robles Gil/Minden Pictures), 21cr (Michael Durham/Minden Pictures), 24b (Thomas Marent/Minden Pictures); Shutterstock: cover and title page; 4cl (Puwadol Jaturawutthichai), 4br (Alen thien), 5tr (Giedrilius), 5cl (David Bokuchava), 5br (Dennis van de Water), 6cr (Fabio Maffei), 6br (Savo Ilic), 7br (Maquiladora), 8–9 (reptiles4all), 8br (Park Ji Sun), 10–11 (AR Pictures), 10br (VectorShow), 13cr & 31bl (Abhindia), 13br (RinArte), 14c (EcoPrint), 14br (Maquiladora), 15cr (Hector Ruiz Villar), 16–17 (Alberto Chiale), 16bl (Choke29), 17tr (SaveJungle), 18–19 (Shane Myers Photography), 18c (Martha Marks), 19tr (Dream_master), 20bl (Eduard Kyslynskyy), 21br (VectorShow), 22–23 (Hinna), 22cl & 32br (Cathy Keifer), 22br (VectorShow), 23cr (reptiles4all), 24–25 (Michael Fitzsimmons), 24tr (Sergey Uryadnikov), 25tr (SaveJungle), 26tr (Kazakov Maksim), 26tl (reptiles4all), 26cr (jaiman taip), 26bl (Joseph), 26br (Johan Larsen), 27tl (tristan tan), 27tr (Katiekk), 27cl (Luke Wait), 27br (GUDKOV ANDREY), 27bl (Sandy van Vuuren), 28cl (Rich Carey), 29tr (FJAH), 29bl (Ery Azmeer).

CONTENTS

Introduction 4
Reptiles and Amphibians 6
Venomous Snakes 8
Constrictors 10
Frogs 12
Toads 14
Salamanders 16
Turtles 18
Chameleons 20
Lizards 22
Crocodilians 24
Fun Facts 26
Your Questions Answered 28
Glossary 30
Further Information 31
Index 32

Introduction

An animal is a living organism made up of cells. It feeds, senses, and responds to its surroundings, moves, and reproduces. Scientists have identified nearly nine million species of living animals, but there are many more to be found.

Life Appears

Single-celled life forms appeared around four billion years ago. Sponges—the first animals—appeared a billion years ago. Over time, more complicated animals evolved and some also became extinct. Dinosaurs were the dominant land animals for 165 million years before they died out 65 million years ago.

Rhinoceros hornbills are birds that live in Southeast Asian rain forests. Birds are warm-blooded animals with backbones. They have wings and most can fly.

Fossilized skull of the dinosaur *Tyrannosaurus rex*

Leaf beetle, an insect

Classifying Life

Scientists organize living things into groups with shared characteristics. The two main kinds of animal are ones with backbones (vertebrates) and ones without (invertebrates). Arthropods make up the biggest invertebrate group. They have segmented bodies and jointed limbs. Insects, spiders, and crabs are all arthropods.

Warm- and Cold-Blooded

Most animals are ectothermic, or "cold-blooded." Their body temperature is controlled by their environment. Mammals and birds are endothermic, or "warm-blooded." Their bodies can generate their own heat, so they can survive in much colder habitats.

Musk ox, a mammal

Langurs in a city

Fragile Earth

We are lucky to share our world with an extraordinary richness of animals. It is important to protect our wildlife. When humans pollute or damage the environment, we harm both animals and people. The future is in our hands.

Animal Habitats

The place where an animal lives is called its habitat. Animals have evolved to inhabit just about every environment on Earth, from tropical rain forests and coral reefs to deserts, mountaintops, and ice floes. They even survive in cities.

Giant leaf-tailed gecko, vulnerable because of habitat loss

5

Reptiles and Amphibians

Reptiles and amphibians are both animal groups that are vertebrates (have backbones) and cannot make their own body heat (are "cold-blooded" or ectothermic). Reptiles include lizards, alligators, crocodiles, turtles, and snakes. Amphibians include frogs, toads, and salamanders.

Water and Land

Amphibians spend their early life in water, breathing through gills, then develop lungs and live on land. Their name means "two lives." Amphibian skin is thin, but reptiles have scaly, watertight skin. Most reptiles live on land and they all use lungs to breathe air—even sea turtles. "Reptile" comes from the Latin word for "crawling."

Metamorphosis

Almost all amphibians undergo a change, or metamorphosis. With its gills and fishy tail, a tadpole looks nothing like its parents. At five weeks its back legs sprout and by ten weeks, the froglet has front legs and a shorter tail. By 14 weeks, it looks like a tiny frog.

The caecilian is a strange, worm-like amphibian. Most species live underground. They use their needle-sharp teeth to eat worms, termites, and even snakes, frogs, and lizards.

Frog larvae (young) are called tadpoles. They do not have legs yet but they have a tail that helps them to swim.

A few reptiles give birth to live young, but most lay eggs. The eggs are soft, like thick paper. This hatchling is a green iguana.

GREEN IGUANA
IGUANA IGUANA

Habitat: Forests; Central and South America
Length: Male 5.9 feet (1.8 m); female 4.9 feet (1.5 m)
Weight: Male 9 pounds (4 kg); female 6.6 pounds (3 kg)
Diet: Leaves, flowers, fruit
Life span: Up to 20 years
Wild population: Unknown; Least Concern

7

Venomous Snakes

Some snakes paralyze or kill their prey by injecting it with venom. Venomous snakes include cobras, vipers, rattlesnakes, and death adders. They are smaller than constrictors (snakes that kill by squeezing), but they can move fast. The black mamba hits 12 miles (20 km) per hour!

Deadly Killers

Australia is home to some of the world's most venomous snakes: tiger snakes, taipans, and brown snakes. Other deadly species include kraits, sea kraits, and sea snakes. Sea snakes inhabit warm, tropical oceans. They breathe air but spend their lives in water.

The banded sea krait's black and yellow stripes warn that it is extremely venomous.

Many vipers have heat-sensing pits that detect prey's body heat. Bush vipers do not have these pits.

BUSH VIPER

ATHERIS SQUAMIGERA

Habitat: Forests; Central Africa
Length: Male 25.6 inches (65 cm); female 27.6 inches (70 cm)
Weight: Male 0.9 pounds (400 g); female 1.4 pounds (650 g)
Diet: Birds, reptiles, rodents, amphibians
Life span: Up to 20 years
Wild population: Unknown; Vulnerable

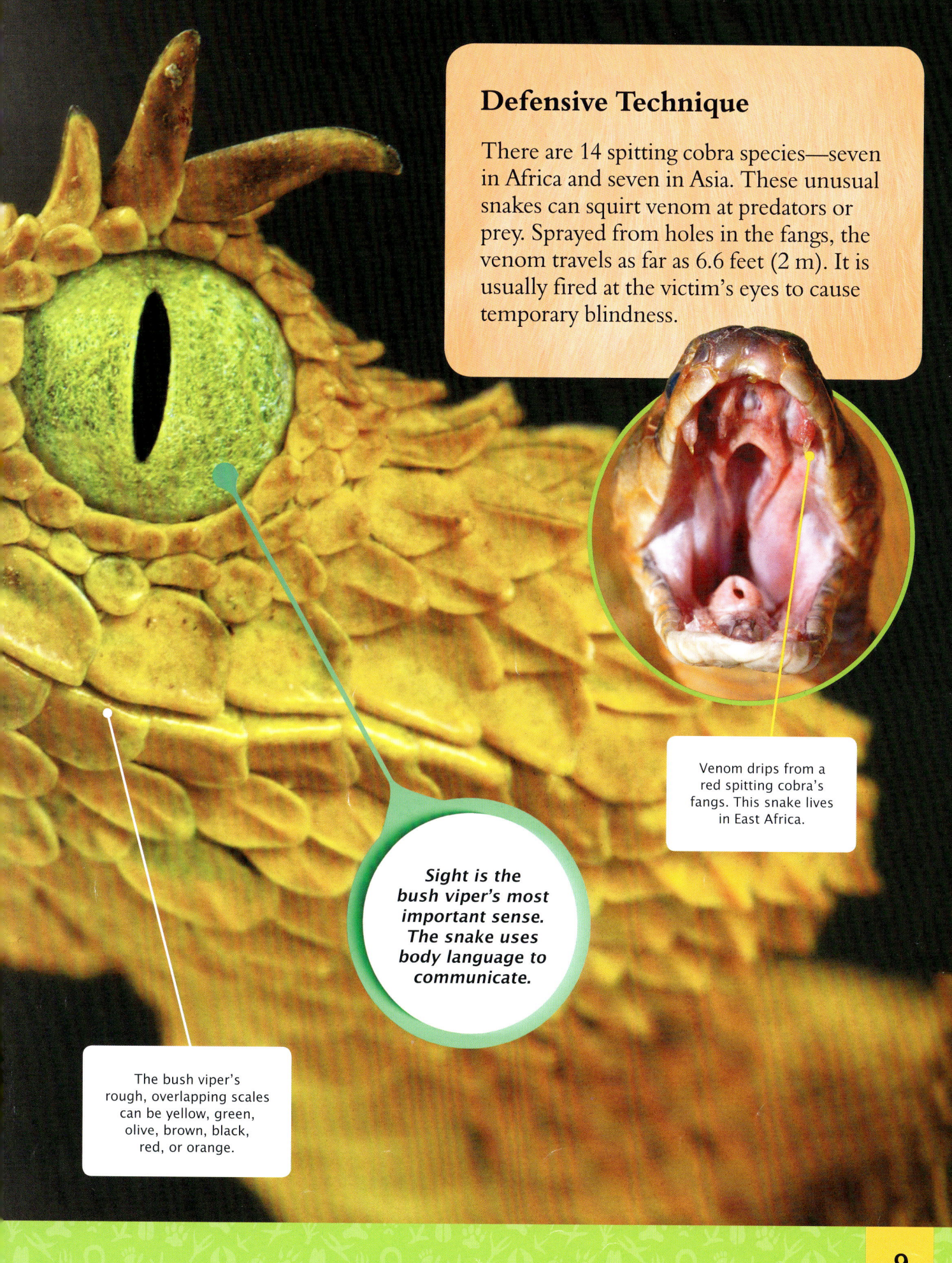

Defensive Technique

There are 14 spitting cobra species—seven in Africa and seven in Asia. These unusual snakes can squirt venom at predators or prey. Sprayed from holes in the fangs, the venom travels as far as 6.6 feet (2 m). It is usually fired at the victim's eyes to cause temporary blindness.

Venom drips from a red spitting cobra's fangs. This snake lives in East Africa.

Sight is the bush viper's most important sense. The snake uses body language to communicate.

The bush viper's rough, overlapping scales can be yellow, green, olive, brown, black, red, or orange.

Constrictors

Constrictors live in the tropics and include boas, pythons, and anacondas. These snakes do not kill their prey with venom. Instead, they coil around their victim's body and squeeze tightly until its blood stops flowing. This cuts off vital oxygen from the heart and brain and the prey quickly dies.

Slow Food

Most snakes are ambush predators that lie in wait rather than actively hunt. They digest their food slowly and may not eat again for months after a big meal. Being cold-blooded, snakes do not use up energy making their own body heat. They spend most of their time resting.

Mature, heavy boa constrictors hide among the leaves on the rain forest floor. Younger ones ambush their prey from trees.

Like most snake species, female green tree pythons are slightly larger than the males.

The green tree python only turns green when it is about a year old. It is born bright yellow, orange, or red.

GREEN TREE PYTHON

MORELIA VIRIDIS
"GREEN PYTHON"

Habitat: Rain forests, scrub; Southeast Asia, Northern Australia
Length: Male 4.9 feet (1.5 m); female 6.6 feet (2 m)
Weight: Male 2.4 pounds (1.1 kg); female 3.5 pounds (1.6 kg)
Diet: Small mammals, reptiles
Life span: Up to 20 years
Wild population: Unknown; Least Concern

10

The python bites its prey before constriction, but its saliva contains no venom.

A resting tree python coils its body over a branch and places its head in the middle.

Big Meals

Snakes' teeth are for gripping food, not for chewing. They swallow prey headfirst and whole. Snakes' jaws have elastic ligaments so they can stretch really wide. Anacondas—the world's heaviest snakes—take the largest prey animals. They catch and eat deer and even jaguars.

Anacondas lurk in swamps and lakes with just their eyes above the water. This one is swallowing an iguana.

Frogs

Frogs are by far the most common kind of amphibian—there are around 4,800 different species. They range in size from a tiny 0.3-inch (7 mm) frog that lives on the floor of Papua New Guinea's rain forests (and holds the record for smallest vertebrate) to Africa's 12.6-inch (32 cm) goliath frog.

Frogs on the Move

Most frogs are strong swimmers and exceptional jumpers. Their legs have stretchy muscles that are pulled in when the frog is at rest. If an enemy approaches, the legs kick back and the muscles act as a spring to push the frog through the air.

The frog has a large, sensitive ear behind each eye. It has sharp hearing.

Frogs jump horizontally rather than up into the air. Many species can leap more than 20 times their own body length.

The tree frog has sticky pads at the end of its fingers and toes for extra grip.

A frog blinks when it swallows its food. This pushes its eyes into the head, forcing the struggling insect down the frog's throat.

Skin Deep

Poison dart frogs live in Central and South American rain forests and come in eye-catching blues, reds, greens, oranges, yellows, and blacks. Their bright skin is a warning to predators that it tastes bad and contains toxic chemicals. The most poisonous, the golden poison frog, contains enough toxin to kill up to 20 people.

Bulging eyes can see about 280 degrees all around. This is useful because the frog cannot bend its neck.

Poison dart frogs are tiny. The largest species, the dyeing dart frog, is just 2 inches (5 cm) long.

RED-EYED TREE FROG

AGALYCHNIS CALLIDRYAS
"BEAUTIFUL SHINING TREE NYMPH"

Habitat: Rain forests; Central America
Length: Male 2 inches (5 cm); female 3 inches (7.5 cm)
Weight: Male 0.3 ounces (10 g); female 0.5 ounces (15 g)
Diet: Small insects, other invertebrates
Life span: Up to 5 years
Wild population: Unknown; Least Concern

13

Toads

The cane toad has a bony ridge across the top of the eyes and snout.

Toads are frogs that have dry skin with warty bumps, instead of the usual moist, smooth skin. They can live farther away from water than other frogs. Toads also move differently—crawling, rather than hopping—and do not have such bulging eyes. The smallest toad is North America's 1.3-inch (3.3 cm) oak toad.

Croak Chorus

Like all frogs, toads must lay their eggs in water. In the breeding season males travel to lakes, ponds, and rivers. They advertise for mates with croaky calls, amplified by an inflatable sac of skin beneath the throat. The croaking attracts nearby females. Big pools can contain hundreds of male toads that croak all night long.

The guttural toad is named for the male's call (guttural means "throaty" or "harsh-sounding"). It is common across sub-Saharan Africa.

CANE TOAD
RHINELLA MARINA
"SMALL-NOSED FROM THE SEA"

Habitat: Grasslands, farmland, scrub; Central and South America, Australia
Length: Male 5.5 inches (14 cm); female 7.9 inches (20 cm)
Weight: Male 1.2 pounds (550 g); female 2 pounds (900 g)
Diet: Rodents, reptiles, amphibians, invertebrates
Life span: Up to 15 years
Wild population: Unknown; Least Concern

The large poison gland on the shoulder produces bufotenin, a toxin that is fatal to many animals.

Eggs, Tadpoles, and Toadlets

The female toad lays thousands of eggs in long strings that wind around plants at the margins of the pool. The tadpoles hatch after a week or two and stay in the water for four to six weeks. By then they have metamorphosed (changed) into toadlets that can survive on land.

Native to the Americas, the cane toad was introduced to Australia and other places to control sugarcane beetles. Unfortunately it is now a threat to local wildlife.

The male midwife toad wraps strings of fertilized eggs around his back legs to keep them safe. When they are about to hatch, he takes them to a pool.

The cane toad has dry, warty skin. Its back toes are partly webbed, but the front ones are not.

Salamanders

Salamanders have slim, lizard-shaped bodies with short legs and long tails, but they are not reptiles—they are amphibians, like frogs. They can survive on land or in water. There are more than 500 species, including newts. Salamanders are the only vertebrates that can regrow a lost leg.

Scary Skin

Their showy skin warns predators that salamanders taste unpleasant and are toxic. All species ooze some kind of toxin from their skin and some are highly poisonous. The rough-skinned newt, which lives in North America, contains a poison that can be fatal to humans, called tetrodotoxin.

A slender body is the perfect shape for spending the day hidden under a rock, log, or pile of leaves.

The fire salamander is named for its markings, which resemble flickering yellow or orange flames.

The poison glands on the emperor newt's back look like orange warts. They contain enough toxins to kill 7,500 mice!

The fire salamander flicks out its tongue to catch worms, slugs, spiders, and insects.

16

FIRE SALAMANDER

SALAMANDRA SALAMANDRA

Habitat: Damp forests; Europe
Length: 7.9 inches (20 cm)
Weight: 1.4 ounces (40 g)
Diet: Worms, slugs, insects, other invertebrates
Life span: Up to 40 years
Wild population: Unknown; Least Concern

Long, flat tail moves from side to side when the salamander swims or runs.

Roughened skin on the toes gives the salamander a better grip on slippery rocks or leaves. Some newts have webbed back feet.

Forever Young

Most amphibians spend their larval stage in water and then lose their gills to live on land as adults. The axolotl never loses its gills. This salamander, which is native to Mexico, stays in water all its life. The axolotl is critically endangered because of habitat loss and pollution.

The axolotl has three pairs of feathery gills. It uses them to collect oxygen from the water.

17

Turtles

Turtles make up a family called chelonians—reptiles that have a protective shell of bone or cartilage. Ones that live in water have flippers for swimming. Turtles that live on land, often known as tortoises, have four short, powerful legs. Like all reptiles, chelonians cannot make their own body heat.

Tiny magnetic crystals in the turtle's brain let it use Earth's magnetic field to navigate.

Landlubbers

Tortoises range in size from the Cape speckled tortoise at around 3.5 ounces (100 g) to the Galápagos giant tortoise at more than 880 pounds (400 kg). They live in deserts, semi-arid zones, swamps, and rain forests. They dig deep burrows to avoid extreme temperatures.

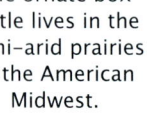

The ornate box turtle lives in the semi-arid prairies of the American Midwest.

Coming Up for Air

Sea turtles usually surface to breathe every five to 40 minutes, but can stay underwater for hours when they are sleeping. Freshwater turtles take a breath every half-hour. Some species, such as the alligator snapping turtle, hibernate through the winter at the bottom of a pond. They hold their breath for months!

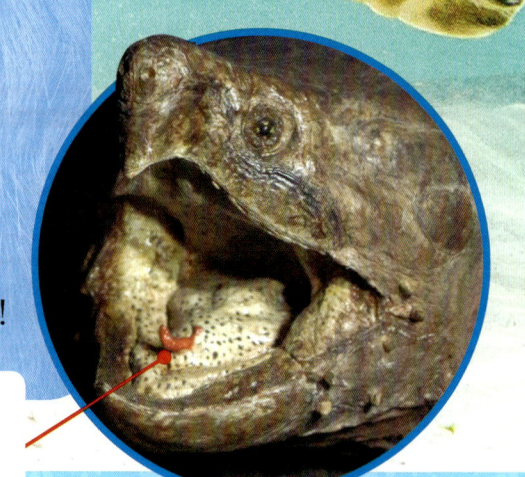

The alligator snapping turtle has a worm-like lure in its mouth that tempts fish to approach.

18

GREEN SEA TURTLE

CHELONIA MYDAS
"WET TORTOISE"

Habitat: Warm oceans; near the equator
Length: 4.3 feet (1.3 m);
Weight: 331 pounds (150 kg)
Diet: Young: jellyfish, marine invertebrates, crustaceans; adults: sea grass, algae
Life span: Up to 80 years
Wild population: Unknown; Endangered

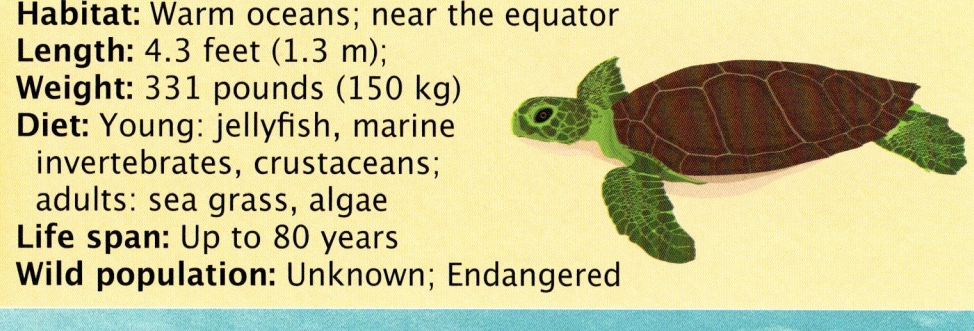

A hard shell of modified bone is covered with plates of keratin (the stuff that makes our nails). It protects the turtle's organs.

The green sea turtle is the second-largest of the seven sea turtle species, after the leatherback.

Paddle-like front flippers power the turtle along. Some green sea turtles migrate 1,300 miles (2,094 km) from their nesting grounds to their feeding grounds.

The sea turtle cannot pull its flippers or its head into its shell.

Chameleons

Chameleons are very specialized lizards that mostly live in trees. There are more than 200 species, of which almost half are found only on the island of Madagascar. Chameleons are famous for being great masters of disguise, but not all species have the special cells that let them change the appearance of their skin.

Unique Eyes

Chameleons are the only animals with two eyes that work independently. One can look forward, while the other looks back, and each eye swivels in all directions. All-around vision helps chameleons to pinpoint the position of fast-moving prey. Most chameleons feed on insects. Larger species, such as Parson's chameleon, also eat lizards and birds.

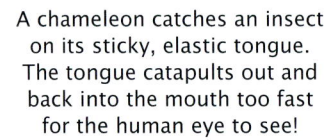

A chameleon catches an insect on its sticky, elastic tongue. The tongue catapults out and back into the mouth too fast for the human eye to see!

20

Chameleons can pick up vibrations but do not have an external ear. Sight is a much more important sense for them.

Quick Change

Chameleons communicate with each other by turning from green to blue, yellow, red, brown, white, or black. They also change in response to the temperature. Turning black can be a sign of nervousness, while yellow can mean the chameleon wants to be left alone.

Green skin indicates to other chameleons that this female veiled chameleon is feeling calm.

Most chameleons have a prehensile tail that acts like a fifth limb. The tail can hold onto branches when the chameleon climbs.

Two toes on one side of the branch and three on the other give the chameleon a secure grip.

PARSON'S CHAMELEON

CHAMAELEO PARSONII

Habitat: Forests; Madagascar
Length: 2 feet (60 cm)
Weight: 1.5 pounds (700 g)
Diet: Insects, other invertebrates
Life span: Up to 7 years
Wild population: Unknown; Near Endangered

21

Lizards

There are more than 6,000 lizard species worldwide (except in very cold habitats). They include iguanas, monitors, geckos, anoles, skinks, and chameleons. Lizards are reptiles that usually have four legs, clawed feet, and a long tail, but there are some legless species.

Dish of the Day

Lizards are varied, and so are their diets. Smaller kinds, such as geckos, feed on crickets, flies, and other insects. Larger ones, such as frilled lizards, also eat small reptiles and mammals. Marine iguanas, the only seagoing lizards, graze on seaweed. The terrifying Komodo dragon kills deer and pigs and also eats carrion.

Glands on the marine iguana's head get rid of all the sea salt it takes in with its food. The short snout and sharp, tiny teeth are perfect for grazing on seaweed and other algae.

Native to rain forests in Southeast Asia, the tokay gecko also enters people's homes. It hunts cockroaches and other invertebrates.

MARINE IGUANA
AMBLYRHYNCHUS CRISTATUS
"CRESTED BLUNT SNOUT"

Habitat: Coastal areas; Galápagos Islands
Length: Male 2.3–4 feet (70–120 cm); female 2–3.3 feet (60–100 cm)
Weight: Male 2.2–29 pounds (1–13 kg); female 1.1–20 pounds (0.5–9 kg)
Diet: Marine algae
Life span: Up to 12 years
Wild population: Unknown; Vulnerable

Dark skin provides good camouflage against the black volcanic rock of the Galápagos Islands.

Defensive Strategies

The frilled lizard scares off predators by unfurling its neck frill and hissing, while the horned lizard's technique is to squirt blood from its eyes! Most lizards, however, run from danger. Many species drop their tail—its violent wriggling distracts the predator while the lizard escapes.

The armadillo lizard rolls into a ball if a predator approaches. It is protected by thick, spiny scales.

Red blotches can appear on the skin in summer. They are caused by pigments in certain seaweeds eaten by the lizard.

23

Crocodilians

Crocodilians are an ancient family of reptiles that appeared during the age of the dinosaurs. As well as crocodiles, they include alligators, caimans, and the gharial. Crocodilians live in and around water worldwide in warm habitats. They are fierce predators.

Man-Eaters

Large crocodilians will eat anything. The saltwater crocodile catches monkeys, deer, kangaroos, and other land animals as well as turtles, sea snakes, and sharks. It has the strongest bite of any animal. It even eats people. Crocodiles carry out hundreds of attacks on humans each year, many of them fatal.

Crocodiles are ambush predators. They may lie in wait for hours before prey comes near. Then they lunge.

Under Threat

The gharial is a critically endangered crocodilian that lives in Asia. There are only around 200 left in the wild. In the past these reptiles were hunted for their skins. Today, many of their river habitats have been dammed. The sand banks where gharials nest are being used by farmers to graze cattle.

The gharial's long, thin snout is too small and weak to take large prey. It has sharp, thin teeth for catching fish.

AMERICAN ALLIGATOR

ALLIGATOR MISSISSIPPIENSIS
"MISSISSIPPI LIZARD"

Habitat: Lakes, swamps; Southern USA
Length: Male 11.2 feet (3.4 m); female 8.5 feet (2.6 m)
Weight: Male 595 pounds (270 kg); female 265 pounds (120 kg)
Diet: Fish, birds, turtles, mammals
Life span: Up to 50 years
Wild population: 5 million; Least Concern

The alligator's snout is wide, rounded, and black. A crocodile's is different—it is narrow, pointed, and olive-green.

The alligator's underside has smooth scales, but its back is covered with bony plates. These protect the alligator and help to disguise it as a floating log.

The alligator has about 80 teeth. When they wear out or break, new ones grow. Over its life an alligator might have 3,000 teeth.

25

Fun Facts

Now that you have discovered lots about different kinds of reptiles and amphibians, boost your knowledge further with these 10 quick facts!

A female frog can produce 20,000 eggs a year. Only one in 100 survives to be an adult frog.

The inland taipan has the most dangerous venom of any reptile. A single bite contains enough toxins to kill 100 people in less than 45 minutes.

The world's longest snake is the reticulated python of Southeast Asia. It can grow up to 30 feet (9 m) long.

Puerto Rico's common coqui frog is the world's noisiest amphibian. Males are just 1.3 inches (3.4 cm) long, but their calls hit 100 decibels.

The female cane toad lays up to 25,000 eggs at once. Each string can be up to 66 feet (20 m) long.

The Chinese giant salamander is the world's largest amphibian. It can be up to 5.9 feet (1.8 m) long and weigh 110 pounds (50 kg).

Tortoises live longer than any other land animal. An Aldabra giant tortoise called Adwaita was a record 255 years old when he died in Kolkata Zoo, India, in 2006.

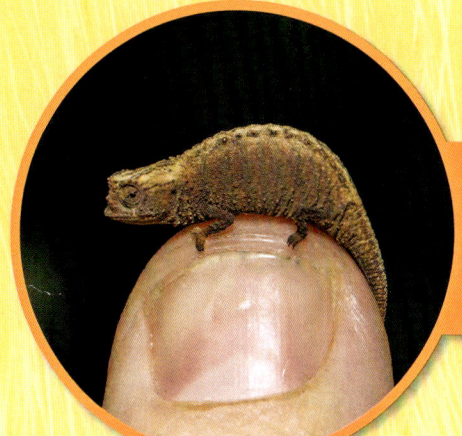

The world's smallest chameleon is a species of leaf chameleon called Brookesia micra. Discovered on Madagascar in 2012, it is less than 1.1 inches (3 cm) long.

The Komodo dragon, a kind of monitor, is the world's largest lizard. It can reach 9.8 feet (3 m) long and weigh up to 154 pounds (70 kg). It also has a venomous bite.

Crocodile hatchlings can only be male if the eggs were kept at around 89.6°F (32°C). Lower or higher temperatures produce females.

27

Your Questions Answered

We know an incredible amount about the creatures that populate our planet—from the deepest oceans to the highest mountains. But there is always more to discover. Scientists are continuing to find out incredible details about the lives of reptiles and amphibians—from their life cycles and migrations to how they hunt and survive. Here are some questions that can help you discover more about these amazing creatures.

How does snake venom work?

Because of the way snakes are built—no legs, arms, or claws to hunt and pin down their prey—venomous snakes are reliant on speed and their deadly saliva to kill prey. Each species produces its own particular venom that works in a way best suited to the snake's needs, but in general, there are three different kinds of toxin used by snakes—cytotoxin, which destroys the prey's body cells and starts the digestion process; hemotoxin, which affects the blood vessels, either destroying them or clotting them; and neurotoxins, which attack the prey's nervous system and paralyze the body.

The prey of the banded sea krait is fish, which means the toxins it uses have to act quickly before the fish can swim away!

Do constrictors have predators?

Despite their size and strength, even constrictors have predators. Young animals are in danger of being attacked by birds of prey, wild dogs, hyenas, frogs, spiders, and even other snakes. Adult constrictors, such as pythons, are particularly vulnerable while digesting a large meal, as they might not be able to move very quickly. Their predators include birds of prey, lions, and leopards.

Why are salamanders poisonous?

All species of salamander are poisonous. They secrete toxins from glands in their skin that cover the body. As most salamanders are otherwise quite defenseless (no claws, thick skin or fur, or sharp teeth), the poison offers important protection. It isn't necessarily a strong toxin (it's usually not dangerous to humans), but at the very least it makes the animal off-putting to potential predators. And because salamander young are particularly vulnerable and defenseless, they often have higher concentrations of toxins on their skin than the adults.

The Iberian salamander has an extra defense mechanism—it pushes its sharp ribs through its skin and coats them in toxins to injure attackers.

Which turtle has the longest migration route?

Most sea turtles migrate throughout the year between feeding grounds and ideal nesting places. They often travel hundreds, even thousands of miles each way. The leatherback turtle travels the furthest each year, swimming 10,000 miles (16,000 km) or more to cross the Pacific Ocean from Asia to the west coast of the United States. Here, it forages for jellyfish before heading back to its nesting grounds. The record-holder for one of the longest migrations ever recorded was a leatherback turtle who swam 12,774 miles (20,558 km) from Indonesia to the US state of Oregon in 2008.

How strong is the bite of a crocodile?

Crocodiles have the strongest bite of any animal. They have specialized in producing an incredible force when snapping their jaws shut, which makes them such effective predators. In a study carried out in Florida in 2012, scientists discovered that the saltwater crocodile holds the record for the strongest bite, slamming its jaws together with a force of 3,700 pounds per square inch (16,460 newtons). In comparison, a human might use a bite force of 150–200 pounds per square inch (890 newtons) when biting off a piece of steak.

The crocodile's jaw muscles are highly specialized to clamp down hard; the muscles that open the jaw, however, are surprisingly weak.

Glossary

ambush predator A hunting animal that waits in one place for prey to come close, rather than hunting by speed or strength.

amphibian A cold-blooded vertebrate that lives in water as a larva and on land as an adult.

camouflage To blend in with one's surroundings.

cold-blooded Unable to keep its own body warm, but rather relying on the environment to heat it (for example by basking in the sun).

flipper A broad, flat limb that many ocean creatures use to move underwater.

gills Slits in the side of an animal's body that help it breathe underwater.

gland An organ in the body that secretes chemicals.

keratin A protein that hair, feathers, hooves, horns, and other body features are made from.

larva (plural larvae) The young stage of an invertebrate that looks different from the adult.

ligament A band of strong tissue that connects the ends of bones or holds an organ in place.

limb A person's or animal's arm or leg; a bird's wing.

mature Fully developed.

metamorphosis The change from one form to another.

paralyze To cause a body to be unable to move.

poison A substance that can damage or kill a living being if injected or swallowed.

prehensile tail A tail that is able to hold or grasp.

prey An animal that is hunted and eaten by other animals for food.

reptile A cold-blooded vertebrate with dry, scaly skin that usually lays soft-shelled eggs on land.

tadpole The larva of an amphibian.

toadlet A very young toad that has just developed from a tadpole.

toxic Either poisonous or venomous.

venom A chemical that is injected into another animal to paralyze or kill.

vertebrate An animal that has a backbone.

Further Information

BOOKS

Jackson, Tom. *Nature's Best: Hunters—How Animals Become the Most Powerful Predators.* London, UK: Wayland Books, 2015.

Mattison, Chris. *Reptiles and Amphibians*. New York, NY: DK Children's, 2017.

McCarthy, Colin. *Reptile*. New York, NY: DK Children's, 2017.

Savage, Stephen. *Focus on Amphibians*. New York, NY: Gareth Stevens Publishing, 2012.

Spelman, Lucy. *Animal Encyclopedia: 2,500 Animals with Photos, Maps, and More!* Washington, DC: National Geographic Kids, 2012.

WEBSITES

Ducksters: Amphibians
www.ducksters.com/animals/amphibians.php
Head to this website to find out all there is to know about amphibians.

Natural History Museum: Reptiles
www.nhm.ac.uk/discover/reptiles.html
This webpage offers lots of video clips and the latest news on reptiles from around the world.

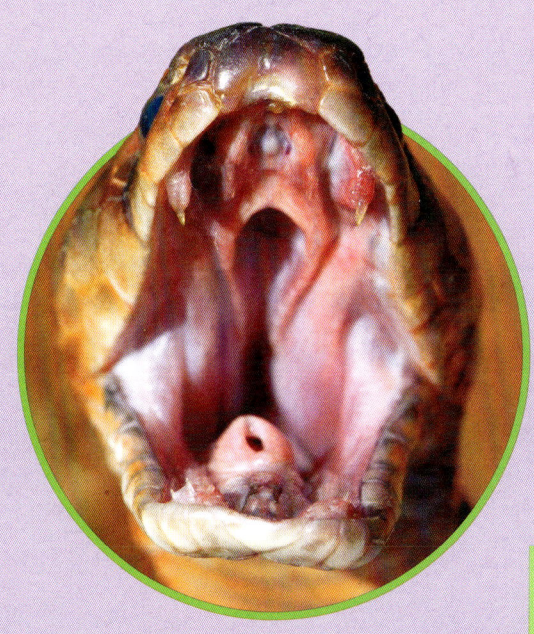

Index

A
alligator 6, 24, 25
ambush 10, 24
amphibian 6–7, 8, 12–13, 14–15, 16–17, 26, 27, 28
anaconda 10, 11
axolotl 17

B
boa constrictor 10

C
camouflage 23
chameleon 20–21, 22, 27
chameleon, Parson's 21
chelonian 18–19
cobra 8, 9
cold-blooded 5, 6, 10
constrictor 8, 1—11, 28
croak 14
crocodile 6, 24–25, 27, 29

D
deadly 8
dinosaur 4, 24

E
egg 7, 14, 15, 26, 27

F
fang 9
flipper 18, 19
frog 6, 12–13, 14, 16, 26, 28
frog, poison dart 13
frog, red-eyed tree 12, 13
froglet 6

G
gecko 5, 22
gharial 24
gills 6, 17
gland 15, 16, 22, 29

H
habitat 5, 17, 22, 24
hatchling 7, 27

I
iguana 7, 11, 22
iguana, marine 22

J
jaw 11, 29

K
keratin 19
Komodo dragon 22, 27

L
larva 6, 17
lizard 6, 16, 20, 22–23, 27

M
Madagascar 20, 21, 27
metamorphosis 6, 15
Mexico 17
migrate 19, 28, 29

P
poisonous 13, 16, 29
predator 9, 10, 13, 16, 23, 24, 28, 29
prehensile tail 21
prey 8, 9, 10, 11, 20, 24, 28, 29
python 10, 11, 26, 28

R
rain forest 4, 5, 10, 12, 13, 18, 22
reptile 6–7, 8–9, 10–11, 14, 16, 18–19, 22–23, 24–25, 26, 27, 28

S
salamander 6, 16–17, 27, 29
snake 6, 8–9, 10–11, 24, 26, 28

T
tadpole 6, 15
toad 6, 14–15, 26
toad, cane 14, 15, 26
toad, midwife 15
toadlet 15
tortoise 18, 19, 27
toxic 13, 16
turtle 6, 18–19, 24, 25, 29
turtle, green sea 19
turtle, leatherback 19, 29

V
venom 8, 9, 11, 26, 28
venomous 8–9, 27
vertebrate 4, 6, 12, 16
viper 8, 9

32